# SUNDAY EXPRESS & DAILY EXPRESS
# CARTOONS

*Seventh Series*

# A DAILY EXPRESS PUBLICATION

01707

Published by the London Express Newspaper Limited, Fleet Street, London, E.C.4 and printed in England by Alabaster, Passmore and Sons, Ltd., London and Maidstone

**4/6**

# Introduction . . . .

GILES has an immense following. His cartoons give joy to millions of " EXPRESS " readers. They are extensively reproduced in the United States and syndicated in the British Empire. They brighten the pages of newspapers at home and abroad. The demand for them is insatiable.

What is the secret ? It is this : Giles has a sardonic humour which appeals because he always keeps close to the life of the street and the farm. He depicts the attitudes of ordinary people.

Ordinary people habitually make caustic comments about high-flown pretension. They are delighted when such comments are made by a man of genius.

Giles debunks the vainglorious. He takes the solemnity out of the grand occasion. He helps the world to keep sane by laughing at its soaring moments.

Giles, though born in North London and beginning as a commercial artist, is of the soil of Britain. He is close to the land. On his farm in Suffolk he breeds a large herd of pedigree pigs. He sometimes links the two professions by making use of his pigs to supply him with models.

I do not need to commend this book. Readers new to Giles—if there are any—have only to turn its pages to know that it contains the work of the master of the comic art.

*Beaverbrook*

Any editor will tell you that there are far more important items in the news than the announcement in this paper yesterday of a new electric iron with a water tank in which you simply add "8 drops of a special perfume—and your linen and lingerie is given the scent of pine or lavender to order." Nevertheless, we are not going to let an opportunity slip by of pointing out the possible dangers of an otherwise splendid aid to hygiene.

*Daily Express, Oct. 16th, 1952*

"Let's hope you don't win one, sir—we look on your old load of junk as our bread and butter."

*Daily Express, Oct. 21st, 1952*

"It has been reported that you left your post yesterday afternoon without permission and went to the Motor Show."

*Daily Express, Oct. 23rd, 1952*

"A gentleman called and sold me two seats for tomorrow's Royal Film Performance—front row
right next to Charlie Chaplin and the Queen."

*Sunday Express*, Oct. 26th, 1952

"You, there—stand to attention when you're returning property to a German officer."

Daily Express, Oct. 28th, 1952

"Gently, copper—lay even yer little finger on me and I could probably get yer a month for assault."

Daily Express, Oct. 31st, 1952

"Looks like a full hut tonight—here come the Republicans with *their* goldamn emblem"

*Sunday Express, Nov. 2nd, 1952*

"I'm VERY interested in their election—if Chuck loses his bet on Eisenhower it's goodbye movies till next pay day."

*Daily Express, Nov. 4th, 1952*

# Preparing for the
# Daily Express Four Day Rally

As a change from rolling 36 feet of mobile studio all over the country, Giles took his $14\frac{1}{2}$ feet of Jaguar XK 120 on a similar journey.

He was entrant No. 258 in the Daily Express Motor Rally, and left from the Norwich starting point. With him went co-driver Ralph Sleigh, who broke the England to Cape Town car record.

Giles holds the St. Ives, Cornwall, record for backing that monster caravan uphill all the way out of St. Ives in the height of the holiday season, leaving the entire town intact.

## IN THE PICTURE

The Giles family children, thinking they were going, too, invited a few colleagues over to his workshop for a final tune-up.

Sleigh (*pictured having his ear oiled*) and Giles (*in overalls*) point out in advance that this was a hazard that the other 460 entrants did not have to face.

*Daily Express, Nov. 7th, 1952*

"Be nice, Butch—explain that it sometimes takes a little time for a Buck Sergeant to get made up to President."

*Sunday Express, Nov. 9th, 1952*

# GILES AND RALPH SLEIGH

## ... TWO SMART MEN GET READY FOR THE RALLY

PREVIEW

FRONT VIEW    OFF-SIDE VIEW    BACK VIEW    NEAR-SIDE VIEW    BIRD'S EYE VIEW

During the Daily Express Motor Rally, Giles and Ralph Sleigh were easily recognisable by their disguise. Great consideration had been given to How to Look Smart Though Fairly Uncomfortable. Appreciating that no one was a real motorist unless he looks like a cross between a deep-sea diver and a village jumble sale, they decided on the same old duffle coats that they wear all the year round, plus a little extra oil and grease.

*Daily Express, Nov. 11th, 1952*

"Grandma, one more gloomy weather forecast because your corns hurt and you won't GET a lift to your sister Fanny in Llanfihangel-Glyn-Myfyr."

*Daily Express, Nov. 12th, 1952*

"Daddy won't love little boys who play motors outside his bedroom the morning after four days' driving in the rally."

*Sunday Express, Nov. 16th, 1952*

The first thing you'll get if they enforce longer hours for shopworkers will be a slight fall in the standard of service.

*Daily Express, Nov. 20th, 1952*

# Marie Stopes and that lower marriage age . . .

And here we have Mrs. Jones, Mrs. Smith, and Mrs. Brown leaving school
ten minutes early to get their husbands' dinners.

*Sunday Express, Nov. 23rd, 1952*

**REHEARSAL ON ICE**

But it will be all right on the actual day—there'll be no ice on the roads, so you won't have the
Guards slipping base over bayonet every time someone calls " 'Alt!'' a bit sharp-like.

*Daily Express, Nov. 25th, 1952*

" 'Tea, SIR?' 'Please, MISS'—and me been drinking tea for two years so's I could get to know her Christian name."

Daily Express. Nov. 27th, 1952

Despondency among the little ones overhearing Father Christmas discussing in very unseasonable terms the suggestion that shopworkers should work longer hours.

*Sunday Express, Nov. 30th, 1952*

"Two hundred tickets to wherever it is he lives."

Daily Express, Dec. 2nd, 1952

"Same as last year, sir—Lads' Club Choral Society accusing the Choir of opening the carol season on their pitch."

*Daily Express, Dec. 4th, 1952*

"Over to you, Miss Markham—and the very best of luck."

Sunday Express, Dec. 7th, 1952

THE GILES FAMILY, circus-bound, in their studio-caravan, have been fog-bound, ice-bound, but have at last reached the circus winter quarters at Ascot where they will be living for a while. Nevertheless, there will be a slight delay with funny jokes about circuses while a certain amount of thawing-out takes place.

*Daily Express, Dec. 9th, 1952*

"Wasn't it kind of those clowns to find us a nice quiet place for tea."

*Daily Express*, Dec. 11th, 1952

"I *thought* there should only be five when I packed them."
(This cost Mr. Mills a new hat for grandma.)

*Daily Express, Dec. 12th, 1952*

"A man said 'Hold these a minute, lady'—
that was two hours ago."

"Mind what you say, Max—that's one of Mr. Giles's
little boys."

*Daily Express*, Dec. 12th, 1952

"The lion-trainer's little boy has been teaching us how to put our heads into the lion's mouth."

*Daily Express, Dec. 13th, 1952*

"Nice piece of suiting, Sidney—very nice."

*Sunday Express, Dec. 14th, 1952*

# HOW GILES SPENT CHRISTMAS

GILES, recovering rapidly from pneumonia, thank you, thought you might like to see how his sickroom looked for Christmas

Here's a key to the carryings-on . . .

1  Healthy friends who heard I was a little better called in to drink my health with my Scotch.

2  Batch of Christmas aunts discussing ailments.

3  Grandma.

4  Another batch of Christmas aunts discussing ailments.

5  Healthy Cousin Andrew, who has a theory that the only cure for pneumonia is to get out in the fresh air and shoot something.

6  Anti-social Christmas aunt discussing ailments on her own.

7  Rush, who ought to have the same theory as Cousin Andrew, but hasn't.

8  Georgie, who has a theory that the more penicillin he pumps into the twins in advance the less chance they've got of catching pneumonia.

9  Me getting a little better.

A plague on your Merry Christmases.

Daily Express, Dec. 27th, 1952

"Stop making holly wreaths, everybody—he's up."

*Sunday Express, Dec. 28th, 1952*

"He said 'Happy New Year' to everyone we met and when they'd gone a little way past he said
'and I hope you fall down a hole'."

*Daily Express, Jan. 1st, 1953*

# BACK TO SCHOOL WEEK —
# by BRITAIN'S MOST FAMOUS CARTOONIST

"Back to School" for me would not mean back to one of your modern rest homes for unretired infants where the children run the teachers.

It would be back to one of the old-fashioned schools that I went to where the teachers ran the children.

Or thought they did.

Back to one of those grey brick boxes on asphalt, where the only useful thing you learned was the art of self-defence during short periods between lessons misnamed "playtime."

"Playtime" took place twice a day. Bang went a bell and out poured hundreds of small boys like a stream of black treacle, the bigger ones lamming into the smaller ones and the smaller ones lamming into the very small ones.

Another bang on the bell announced "playtime" over, and back you all poured into the grey brick box where everybody except the very, very good ones got lammed by the teachers.

When the teachers grew tired of lamming they used the very, very good ones as examples for showing the bad ones up.

## COLLABORATORS

We never seemed able to lay hands on these very, very good ones during playtime because they were always missing.

It has occurred to me since that those who were not creeping about the grey brick box collaborating with the teachers as monitors and prefects were probably using the far corner of the playground as a

*Daily Express, Jan. 13th, 1953*

safety-zone, where they stayed hidden until the end-of-playtime bell gave them the all-clear.

If I went back to school now I should pay more attention to these fifth columnists.

As far as the so-called lessons were concerned, in a class of 50-odd fellow-candidates for delinquency, I expect I should still come out somewhere near the bottom of the exam sheet.

Lessons were instilled into you both ends—by whacking your ear or caning the part you sit down with. They included things like history, geography, art, singing, sums, and most of the accumulated nonsense of the past, with very little reference to the future.

You were reminded every morning about the importance of punctuality by two on each for being late. It was so nice when I left school not to be caned for being late that I have been late ever since.

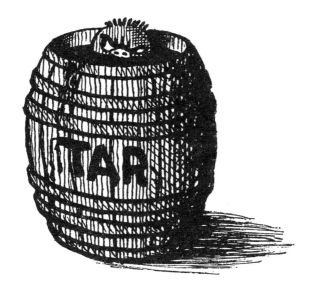

### THOSE DATES !

History meant remembering the dates of battles of the last two thousand years. As I still can't remember the dates of battles for the last two weeks I should still flop at History.

Geography was the names of rivers and volcanoes. I know no more now about (a) rivers and (b) volcanoes than I knew then, except (a) the river that starts at the bottom of my garden and (b) Lord Beaverbrook.

Art. Now there was a subject on which my teachers really used to let themselves go. They gave us a unique variety of things to draw, a cone, a cube, or the eternal green vase which stood next to the tadpole tank on the window sill of every classroom.

*Daily Express, Jan. 13th, 1953*

None of this "Draw what you like" business. The first thing I should organise if I went back to school would be a campaign against all green vases.

Sums. My accountant will tell you that they couldn't have taught me very much about sums. I would still call mental arithmetic brain fever.

Singing. If I thought I should have to suffer another dose of our singing lessons I wouldn't go back.

### 'IF MR. GILES . . .'

The only information we got about the future was to be told how bad it was going to be if we got our name in the punishment book many more times.

But I could go back now armed with the knowledge that they were misinforming us on this count, for I have discovered since that nothing they forecast turned out to be anything like as bad as it is.

Perhaps the only sensible thing they tried to teach us was that it is wrong to smoke.

At 3s. 7d. for 20 they were dead right.

I could tell them they were quite wrong in chastising us for occasionally tarring and feathering the weaker fellow pupil, such things being looked upon nowadays as "self-expression."

Having read enough Hemingway and Dr. Kinsey to know most of the answers, I should know how to come back at that sarcastic old tyrant who lorded it over us for a couple of terms.

When he addressed me with his "If Mr. Giles would kindly come to the front of the class, place the gob-stopper he is sucking in the waste-paper basket, and hand me that intriguing piece of literature he is composing under his desk, I shall be delighted to read it aloud to the rest of the class while he goes upstairs and fetches the cane and book."

Knowing what I know now, I should just sit back and wait for the roar of laughter from my associate scholars to subside and then reply in the modern fashion, without removing my gob-stopper:—

"And if my clever substitute for a teacher doesn't watch his step he will leave me no option but to report him to the education committee and have him flung out on his ear."

It would be interesting to see how the old tyrant reacted to this treatment. I've a pretty good idea.

### MY SYMPATHY

But, apart from the fact that I know I could make it a lot hotter for them now, I don't want to go back.

And lest the teachers of today should think me a trifle biased on the side of the pupils, I hasten to say they all have my deepest sympathy.

Strange as their methods were for passing on the wisdom of the universe, I wouldn't have fancied their chances of coping with the scholars in my part of the world had they not been armed by the authorities with canes, T-squares, bits of chalk to throw at us, and an ability to detect and stamp out any sign of originality before it got serious.

Next: I'm coming over to join the enemy by presenting on the following pages an Alphabetical Guide for Teachers. You needn't buy the paper unless you want to.

*Daily Express, Jan. 13th, 1953*

 GIVES THE A.B.C. OF BACK-TO-SCHOOL WEEK FROM AN OLD BOY'S VIEWPOINT

A for APPLE
offered to teacher.

B for BOYS
which boys will be.

C for CHILDREN.
Most adults think
all children are
lovely. Even the
fact that people
like Hitler were
one of these once
fails to shake their
faith in this popu-
lar misconception.

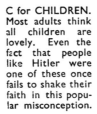

D for DRAWING
PINS. Used for
most things except
drawings.

E for ELASTIC.

F for FAWKES.
You taught 'em
about him.

G for "GOOD"
TYPE. What every
decent type tries
not to be.

H for HERO.

I for IF I were a
teacher I'd get
another job.

J for JOY. Ex-
pression registered
by scholars when
you fall over.

K for KEMISTRY.
See SMELLS.

L for LITERA-
TURE.

M for MOTHERS.
"Do I understand
you 'it my boy?"

N for NASTY
TYPE. Never
looks or smells
very fresh. Every
class has one.

# OVER TO THE ENEMY

O for ORGANIS-ING TYPES. Responsible for nearly all class-room disorders.

P for PAYOFF. The result of all your hard work.

Q for QUIET SORT. Never risk turning your back on these.

R for RUMBLE. Comes from the back of the room when the class is at its quietest.

S for SMELLS. Carbide in your inkwell can account for one of these.

T for TEAM SPIRIT.

U for UNIFORMS.

V for VASE. See this page last Tuesday.

W for WOOD-WORK.

X for WRONG.

Y for YOU. How your pupils see you — and how you think they do.

Z for ZINC. There's the zinc and the zoap. Get cracking.

✓ for RIGHT.

*Daily Express, Jan. 15th, 1953*

"This Churchill-Eisenhower meeting had better come to something—
we've had a big run on 'Winstons' and 'Dwights' lately."

*Sunday Express, Jan. 11th, 1953*

"No, not a Purge—not an S.S. General—not a cosh boy—just Daddy without his keys.
Now be good boys and open the door."

*Sunday Express, Jan. 18th, 1953*

ON THE TRAIL OF THE STURGEON
"Thank you, no—we've had fish once this week."
(This week a sturgeon was presented to Buckingham Palace.)

Daily Express, Jan. 22nd, 1953

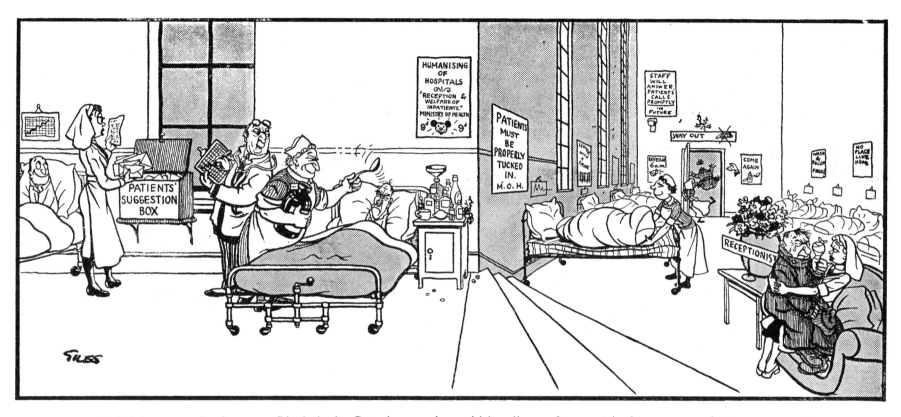

"' Wake up and take your Black Jack, Grizzle-guts,' would hardly conform with the new regulations, nurse."

*Daily Express, Jan. 28th, 1953*

Egad, a T.U.C. leader knighted? Then we shall have knights among the rank and file, forsooth.

*Sunday Express, Feb. 1st, 1953*

"This branded petrol is definitely better than Pool."

*Daily Express, Feb. 4th, 1953*

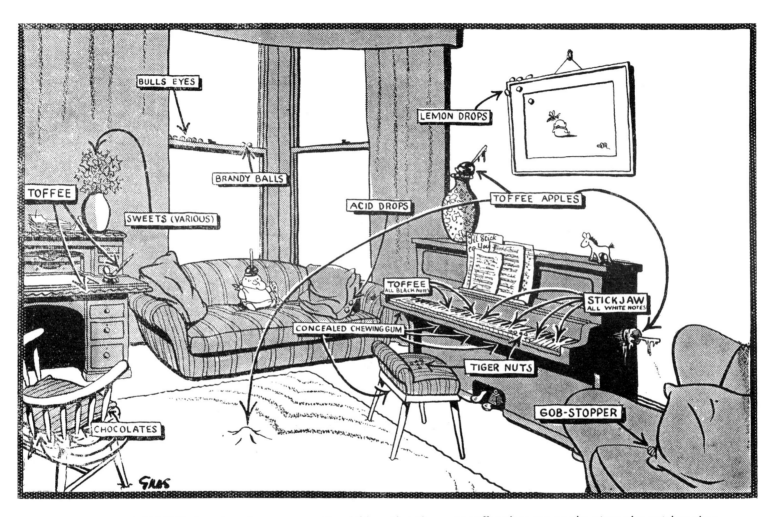

IN THE GILES FAMILY there is a theory among the children that the more toffee they get on the piano the quicker they get their music lessons over—you press one note and they all go down together. I offer this simple sweets-are-now-off-the-ration guide to parents who, during the more or less sweet-free years, may have forgotten the trouble spots.

*Daily Express, Feb. 7th, 1953*

"Archibald reckons they owe him a pint for the time he wasted in the Home Guard waiting for their fathers . . . ."

*Sunday Express, Feb. 8th, 1953*

"That'll teach 'em to write slogans on our coaches."

*Daily Express, Feb. 11th, 1953*

"About time you two quit this Valentine lark."

*Daily Express, Feb. 14th, 1953*

A constable may soon arrest without warrant anyone whom he believes to be carrying an offensive weapon; an offensive weapon is defined as "any article made or adapted to cause injury, or intended by the person having it for such use."

*Sunday Express, Feb. 15th, 1953*

"Now do me another one without the acrobatics, Philip Harben."

*Daily Express, Feb. 17th, 1953*

"Taffy, it don't make no sense ter me—why the 'eck ain't the Welsh wantin' ter speak Hinglish like the rest on us?"

Daily Express, Feb. 19th, 1953

"And for the first time in thirteen years I expect I'll have to buy me own beer."

*Sunday Express, Feb. 22nd, 1953*

The sun shone on the
British for a minute or
two recently.

*Daily Express, Feb. 24th, 1953*

"When I said 'We will all be issued with new weapons by the spring,' 'oo said 'Goodie, goodie'?"

*Daily Express, Feb. 26th, 1953*

"O.K., Honey—if you say it's the 'Mode Boulevard de Pari' I guess it's the 'Mode Boulevard de Pari'."

*Sunday Express, March 1st, 1953*

"Perhaps your Editor would like to come and see the effect his 'Choose a Hat' competition
has had on certain elements of the public?"

*Daily Express, March 3rd, 1953*

"Fog or no fog we're not having the Brigade of Guards striking matches to see if the line's straight."

*Daily Express, March 6th, 1953*

"If he plants 'THE SECOND,' in you all go and get scratching."

*Sunday Express, March 8th,* 1953

"If he raps my head once more with that baton, and says 'Fortissimo,' I'm going to get up and fortissimo him."

*Daily Express, March 12th, 1953*

Mother's Day.

*Sunday Express, March 15th, 1953*

"Three days waiting in this fog for him to arrive—for all we know he may have been and gone."

Daily Express, March 19th, 1953

"How do you spell her second name?"

*Sunday Express, March 22nd, 1953*

It's always an Easter BRIDE we hear about, preparing for her wedding.
Here we have an Easter BRIDEGROOM preparing for his.

Daily Express, March 27th, 1953

"Same old thing every Sunday after the Boat-race—'Please, Mr. Evans, can you get my boy's 'ead out of your fence?'"

Sunday Express, March 29th, 1953

# THE GILES FAMILY LEAVE FOR THE MOON

The Giles Family, in search of a change from its usual week-end by the sea or Easter holiday at the Zoo, has shown enterprise this year by making a space ship.

Whether the moon (240,000 *miles away*) likes it or not, it intends to spend Bank Holiday there.

The following index **may help** you:—

A—Food supplies for Vera.

B—Sunday-best space helmet for Grandma.

C—Drinking water supply.

D—Supplies.

E—Trailer space ship for the twins.

F—George's space helmet gone for a burton.

G—Close-up of moon outfit for the twins, showing details of special landing gear designed by the maker of the "Unknown Political Prisoner."

H—Convoy of fan mail, mostly "Bon voyage, don't come back."

I—Camera to record how half the moon lives. Half because, like most people taking holiday snaps, the Giles Family only gets in half of anything.

J—Television to prove that reception on the moon can't be any worse than it is where they live.

K—The moon having a severe attack of indigestion.

*Daily Express, April 4th and 6th, 1953*

This Giles guide shows why:—1—Rain. 2—Manchester. 3—Moon men queueing to see "What the Butler Saw." 4—The family next door. 5—Moon newsboy. 6—Moon boy burying moon father alive. 7—Moon fathers discussing income tax. 8—Earth grandma and moon grandma sucking bulls'-eyes and discussing rheumatism. 9—Moon children hollering for ice cream. 10—The twins having a go at moon children while they have a chance. 11—Moon children having a go at Vera's boy while THEY have the chance. 12—Father getting booked for parking by moon policemen. 13—Moon man trying to interest George in postcards, carpets, and Easter eggs. 14—Some of the family retiring to the space ship for a cup of tea, and a feeling that they have been to the moon before.

"Your outbreak of peace seems to have caused a few spots, Earthman."

(The Moonmen later attributed the larger spots to Wall-street and areas containing comedians who, faced with a future world without a Russian Aunt Sally, will now have to fall back on jokes about Aneurin Bevan.)

*Daily Express, April 9th, 1953*

"Dad, we've had enough of the Moon and we'd like to get back in time for Silverstone."

Daily Express, May 5th, 195 )

"I think we ought to have asked Mrs. Jones if she minds us leaving our space-ship
in her garden while we are away."

THE GILES FAMILY left today in the mobile studio for Silverstone. They will be sending their annual report of life
in the pits and a vague coverage of the Daily Express International Trophy Race.

*Daily Express, May 6th, 1953*

"O.K., speed fiends—we're off!"

Daily Express, July 17th, 1953

Marshals and stewards got cracking early today clearing the track of night-before arrivals for today's big meeting at Silverstone.

Daily Express, May 9th, 1953

"Spread yourselves—teach 'em there are other things in life besides Silverstone."

*Sunday Express, July 19th, 1953*

"Sh! I heard him telling Mum he's had enough Silverstone for one year so he'll put our motors where we can't get them."

*Sunday Express, May 10th, 1953*

"Come out, darlings, and show Auntie and Uncle the nice little suits Mummy made you for Easter."

Sunday Express, April 5th, 1953

"Vicar! On behalf of the Cornflower Water Colour Group I protest that allowing the Friends of Asia Painting Society to use the village hall the same day as us is carrying peace too far."

*Sunday Express, April 12th, 1953*

"Cave, boys! Shop steward coming up—hide the sweets you've bought with yer tanner orf yer tax."

Daily Express, April 16th, 1953

"I'm just writing Butler a note of thanks for taking the Purchase Tax off pianos and telling him
if he ever needs a flat he can have mine."

*Sunday Express, April 19th, 1953*

"Is that all you're wearing for this bowler?"

Giles drew this cartoon for the menu at a luncheon given yesterday to the Australian Test Cricket team by the London District of the Institute of Journalists.

*Daily Express, April 22nd, 1953*

"Today, boys, I am going to read to you about St. George and the dragon."

Daily Express, April 23rd, 1953

"Sir Winston's not the only one up all night looking after our interests, is he?"

*Sunday Express, April 26th, 1953*

"It's Moscow—say they'd have let us have half a dozen MiGs if we'd gotten them a ticket for the Cup Final."

Sunday Express, May 3rd, 1953

"Converted? Heck, no! They send us here for punishment for being late on parade."

*Daily Express*, May 12th, 1953

" 'Enrietta! You know that advert. you put in the local paper—'Coronation visitors catered for'?"

*Daily Express, May 14th, 1953*

" 'Now let's do it like the Guards would do it,' I think you said, Colonel."

*Sunday Express, May 17th, 1953*

"They said, 'Anything on board there shouldn't be?' and for a joke I said, 'Only the Crown Jewels,' so for a joke they said, 'O.K. there's five minutes before your ship leaves—let's have her down to make sure.'"

Daily Express, May 18th, 1953

"Thought you'd take the micky out of the Guards in last week's Sunday Express then hop off
out of the country for a while, did you?"

*Sunday Express, May 24th, 1953*

"Very well—let's hear YOU explain in YOUR impeccable Spanish that we've promised
Grandma we'll be back in time for the Coronation."

*Sunday Express, May 31st, 1953*

"It's like this, Mother. I thought I'd step up the travel allowance by running a book on the Derby. Unfortunately they all seem to have backed the winner.

NOTE: If there is any truth in the report that Russia intends to welcome tourists, the French Riviera can stand by for some pretty keen competition from those Siberian winters.

*Sunday Express, June 14th, 1953*

"If your swim suit HAS come off in the water, Vera, you'll probably have to stay in until Spain has a change of government."

*Sunday Express, June 21st, 1953*

"My wife's got a theory that it doesn't pay to let them know you're English."

*Daily Express, June 24th, 1953*

"The sooner this family learns that NO ENTRADA on a door in Spain means NO ENTRY the better."

*Daily Express, June 25th, 1953*

"People who take their children for holidays in Spain want to leave them there."

Daily Express, June 30th, 1953

" There's several reasons why you can't finish your game tonight—one because you're not Drobny,
and he's not Patty, and another because you're clearing out and I'm locking up."

*Sunday Express, June 28th, 1953*

FOOTNOTE TO A DAILY EXPRESS READER'S LETTER

*". . . people will not pay for what they do not get—real meat. We get bones, gristle, and fat. To cope with the modern idea of meat we must develop fangs of Alsatian dogs."*

*Daily Express, July 3rd, 1953*

"From there to there—Test Matches. From there to there—Wimbledon. This week we
have the British Open Golf Championship."

*Daily Express, July 7th, 1953*

"Now tell me they don't favour Public Schoolboys at Dartmouth Naval College."

Daily Express, July 9th, 1953

"To the stage, lads—and sorry I am if we do not bash the living daylights out of our opponents with 'Peace, perfect Peace'."

*Sunday Express, July 12th, 1953*

"It's your Mrs. Ramsbottom again—stopping her old man's two bob each way."

*Daily Express, July 21st, 1953*

"Sorry, Hutton—sorry, Compton—sorry, everyone—got to watch they don't start swopping cricketers like race-horses."

*Daily Express, July 23rd, 1953*

"Tell us, Sidney—where've they buried the rest of it?"

*Sunday Express, July 26th, 1953*

# KOREA ARMISTICE

"GENTLY, GENTLY . . ."

*Daily Express, July 28th, 1953*

"WHO can't come out looking like WHAT?"

Daily Express, July 30th, 1953

"And then it goes on to say: 'Even if the Russians haven't got an H-bomb yet they soon will have, and if it isn't bigger than ours it's sure to be just as big and . . ' "

Sunday Express, Aug. 11th, 1953

# THE CASE OF WILLYUM
## *versus* LORD GODDARD

by **GILES** DOMICILE : SUFFOLK

"East Anglians are always awkward and obstinate," said Lord Goddard, referring to an Eastern Counties farmer who slammed the door in the face of a Weights and Measures inspector.

Well, the days went past without incident and we began to think the boy Willyum, not being very hot on literature or reading newspapers, had not got wind of this piece of information handed out by the Lord Chief Justice.

But unfortunately one of the many knights of the road who since the days of Boadicea, East A., have doggedly tried to sell East Anglians merchandise from the pagan countries, happened to tell Willyum all about it just when Willyum was laying down the law at the local about what we ought to do with foreigners who stopped taxes out of his wages to keep Lun'uners

alive and saying that he warnt goin' to pay for no National 'Elth stamps an' nor were he goin' to work overtoym for Farmer who would only stop more taxes out of his wages if he did.

Now to Willyum, who has worked on this farm for 80-odd years and has threatened to give notice every day since we bought a tractor, and who has to be set to work facing the other way while we use the combine in case he sees it, being called "Stubborn and arkward" by one of these 'ere Lun'uners was like waving a red flag to a McCarthy.

Only after a violent struggle ending with about ten of us holding him down while we promised that we'd get Lord Goddard to come and be personally granted a free pardon by Willyum did we prevent a march on London which might well have shaken the very seat of Justice.

*Daily Express, Aug. 6th, 1953*

HOLIDAY CARTOON—Life in a Holiday Camp.

*Sunday Express, Aug. 2nd, 1953*

**HOLIDAY CARTOON—Down on the Farm.**

*Sunday Express, Aug. 16th,* 1953

" HURRAH —

*Daily Express, Aug. 3rd, 1953*

for the Sun! ''

*Sunday Express, Aug. 9th, 1953*

. . . there is nothing—absolutely nothing—half so much worth

doing as simply messing about in boats . . . *Kenneth Grahame*

HOLIDAY CARTOON—Now among the soldiers.

Sunday Express, Aug. 23rd, 1953

HOLIDAY CARTOON—A quiet picnic.

*Sunday Express, Aug. 30th,* 1953

*Daily Express*, Aug. 13th, 1953

"Here's to the jolly old Government loan—and may the strike go on for ever."

"Knock 'is 'at off—like
Lindwall did 'Utton's"

*Daily Express, Aug 18th, 1953*

"Did you win, Bud?"

*Daily Express, Aug. 20th, 1953*

"Good thing, too—but don't tell the old man about it this morning."

*Daily Express, Aug. 27th, 1953*

"I make it five per cent. prefer the new white, five per cent. prefer the old grey, and 90 per cent. don't give a hoot what colour it is."

Daily Express, Sept. 1st, 1953

"Supersonic bang demonstrations are costing me something in glasses."

*Daily Express, Sept. 3rd, 1953*

Postscript to the Electricians' strike.

*Sunday Express*, Sept. 6th, 1953

Several motorists eager to prove just how good they can be used the Daily Express Tour of Britain as an opportunity to strike at their enemy, the cyclists. And as a safety measure against the wrath of cyclists who might resent being called "the enemy," GILES points out "*I am a cyclist—that's me cutting the corner on a trade bicycle*"!

*Daily Express, Sept. 8th, 1953*

"If we had men for husbands they'd make their Mr. Deakin fit them up with little Eskimo suits to go with his wage-freeze policy."

*Sunday Express, Sept. 13th, 1953*

" You've got to hand it to him—hollering all last week at the T.U.C. conference for equal pay for women."

*Daily Express, Sept. 15th, 1953*

" Here he comes—' Mister-my-Dad's-giving-the-biggest-marrer-in-the-parish.' "

*Sunday Express, Sept. 20th,* 1953

" Report me to who you like—my charge is one and six each and three shillings that one at the end."

*Daily Express, Sept. 24th, 1953*

" Telling me they will have bigger bangs than this in Australia next week is of small consolation, O wise one."

*Sunday Express, Sept. 27th, 1953*